They rode like the wind . . .

With a soft whinny of pleasure, Bella turned and
cantered toward the farmyard gate. She checked
and gathered herself and then leapt. Irina hardly
felt the jump. It felt more like flying. Her cold
bare feet clung to Bella's smooth warm sides, and
her fingers entwined themselves in the thick mane,
and they were off like the wind across the wide
snowy fields. . . .

Irina didn't think to wonder where Bella was
taking her. She didn't think of being frightened.
She didn't think of being cold. She didn't think of
anything. She felt the warmth of Bella's galloping
body, the strong thick mane in her fingers, the ever-
increasing speed that lifted her long hair and made
it stream out behind her like the horse's tail. More
than anything else, she felt happy.

THE
ENCHANTED
HORSE

by Magdalen Nabb

illustrated by Julek Heller

Hyperion Paperbacks for Children
New York

SCHOOL BOOK FAIR EDITION

Text © 1992 by Magdalen Nabb.
Illustrations © 1992 by Julek Heller.

First published in hardcover in 1992. Reprinted by permission of Orchard Books.

For information address Hyperion Books for Children,
114 Fifth Avenue, New York, New York 10011-5690.

Printed in the United States of America.

The artwork for this book is prepared using pencil.
The text for this book is set in 14-point Kennerly.

Library of Congress Cataloging-in-Publication Data

Nabb, Magdalen, date.
The enchanted horse / by Magdalen Nabb : illustrated by Julek
Heller. — 1st Hyperion Paperback ed.   p.   cm.
Summary: A lonely young girl living on a remote farm
with her work-obsessed parents
cares for an old and battered wooden horse
with such devotion that it comes to life.
ISBN 0-7868-1107-2
[1. Horses—Fiction. 2. Magic—fiction. 3. Farm life—Fiction.]
I. Heller, Julek, ill. II. Title.
PZ7.N125En   1995
[Fic]—dc20   95-3785

*This book is dedicated to
Maestro Nino Di Fazio
with admiration for his
boundless knowledge of horses.*

One

IT WAS CHRISTMAS EVE, and the afternoon had frozen as hard and milky as a pearl. The sun was as thin and pale as a disk of ice in a sky as white as the snowy ground.

Irina walked in front of her mother and father along the lane that led across the fields to the village. She was dressed in a sheepskin coat and boots and mittens and a sheepskin hat. Her long fair braid hung down behind her. The cold pinched her thin cheeks, and the trees that grew on each side of the lane poked their black fingers through the freezing fog as if they were trying to clutch at her as she went by.

Even before they reached the first houses at the edge of the village, Irina heard the faint sound of a band playing Christmas carols. But she didn't look up and smile or turn to say "Listen!" to her mother and father. She only walked quietly on, looking down at her thick boots as they trod the hardened snow. Irina didn't like Christmas.

When they reached the village, all the shop windows were already lit, making halos of light in the fog. The snow-covered square where the band was playing around the Christmas tree was hung with colored bulbs.

But Irina and her parents didn't stop to listen to the carols, because they had so much to do. They lived on a farm, and at Christmas everyone wants more cream and eggs and milk, and besides, they had to be back home in time to feed the animals. So her father stopped to talk to the dairyman at the corner, and Irina went ahead with her mother to help with the shopping.

They went to the baker's to buy bread and flour and had to wait in a long line. At the front of the line, a girl who was smaller than Irina reached up and pointed at the cakes and little pies sprinkled with sugar.

"And some of those," she shouted, "for Grandma! And the big cake! Grandpa likes cakes! The big cake!"

Irina watched her and listened to every

word, but when it was her mother's turn, she didn't ask for anything. She was thin and never had much appetite, and there was no Grandpa or Grandma coming for Christmas dinner.

They went to the greengrocer's and waited in the long line. A fat little boy with a red scarf wound round and round his neck was quarreling with his older sister.

"I like *dates* best!" he protested.

"No you don't," his sister said. "You only like the box with the picture on it, and we're going to buy figs and nuts and tangerines, so there." And their mother winked at the greengrocer's wife and bought figs and nuts and tangerines and dates.

Irina watched them and listened to every word, but when it was her mother's turn, she didn't ask for anything. She had no brothers or sisters to quarrel with.

The band in the square began to play "O Come, All Ye Faithful," and the fat little boy in the red scarf and his sister joined in the singing as they went out.

It was getting dark, and the colored lights twinkled brighter now against the shadowy snow. On the corner outside the greengrocer's shop, a fat lady with a long apron and thick gloves was selling Christmas trees. A thin boy, taller than Irina, was choosing one with his father. "This one! No, this one—no, that one, *that* one. It's the biggest!"

And his father laughed and said, "And how do you think we'll get it home?" But he bought it, even so, and the fat lady wound some thick string around it to help them carry it.

Irina watched and listened, but she didn't ask for anything. Years ago her mother had said, "You're too old now to be bothering about a Christmas tree. It's a waste of money. You can choose a nice present instead."

So they walked past the Christmas trees and crossed to the other side of the square. There was a toy shop there, and next to that a gloomy junk shop with a bunch of dusty mistletoe hanging in the window, and next to that a shop that sold pretty dresses with full velvet skirts. Irina stood beside her mother and stared at the shop windows with bright eyes, but she didn't ask for anything. What was the use of a party dress when she lived so far from the village that she never went to a party? And what was the use of toys when there were no children near enough to play with?

"Have you thought what you'd like?" her mother asked. "You know we mustn't be long—we've a lot to do."

Irina tried to think. It's nice to be able to choose anything you want, but it's nicer still when your present is a surprise. So she stared at the big dolls in boxes and then at the dresses and then at the tinsel and the silver bells decorating the window. She wanted to choose something that would please her mother.

Then she remembered the fat little boy and his cheerful red scarf, and so as not to keep her mother waiting and make her angry she said, "I like the red velvet dress. . . ."

"And where do you think you'll go in it?" said her mother impatiently.

"I don't know. . . ." It's hard to please your mother when you don't know exactly what she wants you to say. Then she turned and saw her father coming.

"Well?" he said. "Have you finished shopping? It's about time we were getting back."

"Irina hasn't chosen her present," said her mother crossly. "And to look at her face,

you'd think it was a punishment instead of a treat."

Irina wanted to say, "I don't want anything. I'm not asking for anything. I'd rather go home." But she didn't dare.

Then her father said, "Come on. Let's have a look in that toy shop. There must be something you'd like."

"She's spoiled, that's what she is," her mother said. "She doesn't know what it means to want for anything."

The band in the square was playing "Silent Night" very quietly. The sadness of the music, the growing darkness, and the cheerfulness of all the other families made Irina want to cry.

"I don't want anything," she said to herself fiercely. "I don't—" But just as they were coming to the toy shop, she stopped.

"Come on," said her father. "You're not going to find anything there."

But Irina didn't move. She was staring in through the window of the junk shop, trying to make something out in the gloom.

"Irina!" said her mother. "For goodness' sake, we have to get home."

But Irina, always so quiet and obedient, for once took no notice.

"The horse," she said. "Look at the poor horse."

"What horse?" said her father.

"I can't see any horse," said her mother. And they both peered into the gloomy junk shop. Beneath a jumble of dusty broken furniture, they could just make out the head and tattered mane of what was probably a rocking horse.

"I see it now," her father said. "Well, come on—let's get on. You don't want that old thing for Christmas."

"I should hope not," her mother said. "It looks filthy."

But Irina stared up at them bright-eyed, and the tears that had started with the sad carol and the growing darkness and the cheerfulness of all the other families spilled over and ran down her cheeks.

"It's being crushed," she cried. "It's lonely and frightened and being crushed under all those things!" And before her parents could stop her, she had run inside the shop, and all they could do was follow her.

Two

ONCE INSIDE, IRINA STOOD STILL, wondering what to do. She'd never seen such confusion in a shop before. It didn't really look like a shop at all, but more like the untidiest house in the world. The piles of old furniture reached right up to the ceiling, and it was difficult to pass between them. There were ornaments, too, and brass buckets and lamp-stands and old stoves and typewriters and objects you couldn't tell the use of, and everything was thickly coated with dust, including the one bare light bulb that left most of the room in shadow.

"What can I do for you?" asked a voice in the gloom.

Irina looked about, but she could see no one. She felt frightened, but she stood where she was and waited.

"Anyone at home?" said her father's voice behind her.

A voice chuckled. "I am," it said, "if you want to call this home. Past the big dresser on your left."

Irina looked around. At first she could make nothing out, but then she noticed a huge armchair with carvings on it as big as a throne, and the profile of a man's head just visible.

"See me now?" But the head didn't turn and the eyes were shut. "I suppose it's getting dark, but I can't see and I don't know why I should pay out good money so that others can see. There's nothing much worth looking at, though I make a living after a fashion. What was it you wanted?"

"The rocking horse," Irina said, as loudly as she dared, and she went closer to the huge carved chair. The man seated there was almost as small and slight as herself, and his closed eyes were sunk in his white face, so that he seemed to have no eyes at all. He wore a black smock, and his pale hands rested on his knees as quietly as mice.

"Irina . . . !" protested her mother in an

angry whisper. Irina stood where she was, her fists clenched in fear and determination.

"She saw the horse in the window—" Irina's father began, but the blind man took no notice of him.

"What's your name?" he asked, his face lifted toward Irina.

"Irina."

"Irina," he whispered. "Come closer to me."

Irina was frightened of the blind man, but she had to rescue the horse. She went closer. The blind man lifted his mouselike hands and touched her face, feeling her eyes, her thin cheeks, her mouth, and her chin in turn.

"Irina," he said again, and he patted her face gently. "You're a very sad little girl. Why don't you play and be happy?"

"Because there's nobody to play with," Irina said.

"And that's why you want Bella? To play with?"

At first Irina didn't answer because she didn't know who Bella was, but then she thought and said, "Is Bella the name of the horse in the window?"

"That's right," said the blind man.

"Then I don't want her to play with," Irina said boldly. "I want to look after her because she's dirty and lonely and crushed under all those heavy things in your window."

"In that case," said the blind man, "you'd better take her home with you."

Irina stood still and waited, wondering if her mother would say she couldn't, but nobody spoke until the blind man said, "Would you like to know why I call her Bella?"

"Yes," said Irina. "Did she belong to another girl who called her that?"

"I don't rightly know," the blind man said, "who she belonged to, but I'll tell you her story, such as it is. Do you remember a wicked farmer who used to live hereabouts who was known as Black Jack?"

"No," said Irina, "I don't."

"Well, well," said the blind man, "you're very young and it was all before your time."

"I remember him," said Irina's father, coming closer. "He kept horses."

"He did," said the blind man. "And the most beautiful one of all was named Bella because Bella means 'beautiful.' But he was an evil man and treated his animals badly, very badly. They never got more than a handful of oats a day, barely enough to keep them alive, and Bella, who was as finely bred and elegant as a racehorse, was forced to pull him around in that dirty old cart of his. They say he whipped her until she bled. No one knew where he got her, but some said he captured her himself from a wild herd that sometimes passes by this way."

"And what happened to her?" Irina asked.

"I don't know," the blind man said. "But I can tell you what happened to Black Jack. He died."

"I remember," said Irina's father. "I went to the auction when his farm was sold. My old father was still alive then, and he kept a pony and trap himself. It was he who talked me into going, but there was little enough worth buying, and the horses were only fit for the slaughterhouse."

"Even Bella?" asked Irina.

"Bella wasn't there," the blind man said. "Bella wasn't there. I asked about and I spoke to the auctioneer himself, but there was no horse of that description on his list. Poor creature. Poor beautiful creature. . . ."

The blind man fell silent with his thoughts as if he'd forgotten there was anyone there.

"Was she dead, then . . . ?" whispered Irina after a while.

"I bought all that stuff in the window from Black Jack's place," the blind man said, without giving her an answer, "and there it's been ever since, including the horse."

"Now, what would Black Jack have wanted a rocking horse for?" wondered Irina's father. "He had neither wife nor child."

"But that's just it," said the blind man very softly, just as if he were talking to himself. "It's not a rocking horse."

Then he spoke more loudly, turning his face up toward Irina's father's voice.

"Take the horse home for your little Irina," he said. "If it will make her happy, I don't want anything for it. Only perhaps you'll have to come for it another day when the boy who helps me is here. You understand. I can't move all that stuff to get at it."

"That's very nice of you," said Irina's father. "We'll call another time."

He took Irina by the shoulder, but Irina, who never asked for anything, cried, "Please! Please, can we wait in case he comes?" And she touched the blind man's arm, no longer afraid of him. "*Please* let us wait! You can tell us more stories about Bella."

"Come on, now," said her father, and he led her to the door. "You know we have to get home."

"And don't imagine we're coming back," warned her mother as they went. "That filthy thing must be a mass of woodworm, and it's not coming into the house."

Outside on the snowy pavement Irina began to cry. The band was still playing around the Christmas tree, and the people had finished their shopping and were starting for home, loaded with packages and calling to one another under the winking lights.

"Merry Christmas! Merry Christmas to you!"

Before her parents could take her away, Irina turned her tearful face for a last look at Bella's poor head, crushed under all that junk, and then from inside the shop the blind man's voice called out, "Stop!"

It was as if he had given an order that had to be obeyed. Irina's parents hesitated and looked at each other.

"Come back a moment, if you will."

Irina's father shrugged. "I suppose we'd better see what the poor old chap wants."

They went back inside the gloomy shop, and Irina ran straight to the blind man's chair. He was sitting just as they'd left him, with his hands resting quietly on his knees.

"I never mistake a footstep," he said. "When you can't see, you learn to recognize people in other ways." Then he lifted his face up and called, "Hurry up, now! We have customers waiting!"

Irina turned around and saw a tall, cheerful boy come in from behind where her parents stood watching.

"I came to wish you Merry Christmas, Granddad!"

The grinning boy spoke at the top of his voice as though the man were deaf rather than blind.

"And just as well you did," said the blind man. "There's a job for you to do. This is Irina, and she wants to take Bella home with her, so you'll have to get her out from under all that stuff in the window."

"Right you are, Granddad!" said the boy.

"I don't think . . . ," began Irina's mother, but the boy had already climbed into the window and was heaving the broken furniture about.

"I'll have her out of here in two minutes!"

"Is he your grandson?" asked Irina shyly.

"No," said the blind man, "but that's what he likes to call me."

"I haven't got a granddad," Irina said, and she stared at the blind man, wishing he were her granddad, because he could make her parents do what he told them.

"Here you are!" said the boy, and he set Bella down on the floor by Irina. She touched the dirty, tangled mane timidly.

"Your father will carry her home for you," the blind man said. "She's too heavy for you."

And sure enough, without a word of protest, Irina's father came and picked up Bella.

"She's a fair weight," he said, "but I'll manage."

"I'll help you," Irina said.

"You help your mother carry the shopping," said her father. Irina followed him to the door, holding her breath because she could hardly believe they were really taking Bella away. But once they were outside, she remembered something and ran back.

"Thank you," she said to the blind man. "And thank you for getting Bella out for me," she said to the cheerful boy, who was perched on the arm of the huge chair, swinging his long legs.

"Good-bye, Irina, and Merry Christmas," said the old man, and he lifted his small white hands toward her. She went closer, understanding now that he needed to touch her because he couldn't see her. "Be happy," he said gently, and patted her cheek.

"I will be happy," Irina promised, "and I'll look after Bella—and can I ... can I come back and see you one day?" She would have liked to ask him if she could call him Grand-dad, as the boy did, but she didn't dare.

"Come whenever you like," said the blind man. "I'm always here."

"Merry Christmas!" she whispered, her eyes shining, and she ran outside.

Three

ALL THE LONG WAY HOME, Irina's mother had a lot to say about moths and woodworm and dirt not coming into her clean house, but Irina hardly heard her, she was so happy, and by the time they reached the farm it had been settled that Bella should be put in the old barn, which in any case was already half-full of junk, where she would dirty nothing and be in nobody's way.

"Can we put straw down for her?" Irina asked as Bella was carried in.

"You can do as you like," her father said. "But you'd better change into your old clothes first, or you'll have your mother after you." And he stood Bella in a corner of the barn just inside the door.

"Let me just look at her first," said Irina. "I won't touch her—I just want to look."

They both looked. It was a sorry sight. There was no telling what color the horse was meant to be because she was so thickly coated with dirt. Her mane and tail seemed to be of real horsehair, matted, tangled, and filthy. It was difficult to tell just what she was made of, but it was true, as the blind man had said, that she wasn't a rocking horse. She stood square on her four hooves, and there was nothing to suggest that she had ever had rockers. Her head drooped a little, and her eyes under the tattered mane were squeezed almost shut, as though she were crying.

"Poor creature," whispered Irina, imitating the blind man's words.

"Come on. We've got work to do," her father said, slapping the dust from his hands and coat. "Get changed and start collecting the eggs. We're late with the milking."

Irina was used to working hard on the farm, and since there were no children around to play with, she never minded it. But that evening she worked twice as fast as usual so that she would have time to visit Bella before supper.

She ran so fast with the heavy baskets of

eggs that if she didn't break any, it was only because she was lucky not to slip on the icy stones of the farmyard, and it was a wonder that she didn't give the hens cattle cake to eat by mistake.

Even so, by the time she had finished all her chores, there was only time to lay down some fresh straw for Bella before her mother called.

"Irina! Come and lay the table—supper's ready!"

"I have to go in," Irina whispered to Bella, stroking the poor tangled head. "But tomorrow I'll come and see you before we go to church, and afterward I'll brush and comb you and talk to you so you won't be lonely."

"Irina!"

She turned off the light and went into the house.

Because there was some extra cooking and baking to help with for the next day, it was late when Irina went up to bed. In her nightdress, she sat on the bed and wrapped up the little presents she had made at school for her mother and father. She was so happy that they had let her have Bella that she would have liked to give them something bigger and better, but there was nothing she could do about it now. Perhaps she could think of an extra chore to do tomorrow to help her father. And if she said she was hungry and ate more than usual, her mother would be pleased. She always looked worried and cross when Irina left food on her plate.

When the presents were tied and ready, Irina put them on the chair by the bed. But

she felt too excited to go to sleep and went
to look out of her window where one of the
apple trees that grew in the yard almost
touched the panes with its bare branches. It
was too dark to see the old barn properly,

but Irina stood there a long time with her head pressed against the glass, thinking of Bella and listening to the faint noises of the cold night.

And in the darkness of the barn with the clean straw spread around her, Bella stood with her head lowered and her eyes half-closed as though she, too, were listening.

Four

IRINA WAS THE FIRST TO WAKE on Christmas morning. Dawn hadn't broken, and the house was hushed and dark. She wrapped herself up warmly and tiptoed down the stairs and out across the icy yard to the old barn.

"Bella!" she called softly as she pulled the big door open and switched on the light. "Bella! It's Christmas. . . ."

Her eyes shone with pleasure as she approached the horse and reached out to touch the stiff ears and tangled mane.

"Don't be sad," she said gently. "You won't be lonely anymore now, because I'll come every day and talk to you and brush you and give you clean straw."

She knelt beside Bella and lifted the matted mane from her sad eyes.

"I'll find you an old blanket, too, if I can, because the nights are so cold. And then in the spring I'll take you outside in the meadow, where there'll be grass and flowers and a stream for you to drink from. Will you like it? Will you, Bella?"

She would have liked to put her arms around Bella's neck and hug her tight to make her sadness go away, but she was still shy of her. Instead she promised, "After Christmas dinner I'll be able to stay with you all afternoon, and I'll wash and comb you so you'll look beautiful."

Then she got to her feet and tiptoed to the door. Before she switched the light off, she said, "Merry Christmas, Bella."

Out in the yard it was still dark. Irina mixed some mash for the hens as a surprise for her father. Then she washed her hands in the dairy and pulled off her boots to go in and lay the table for breakfast as a surprise for her mother. They were surprised, but not because she'd done the extra work. Her father gave her a pat on the head and said, "Well! You look as bright and cheery as a robin this morning. What's come over you?"

Her mother, watching her eat her breakfast quickly, looked puzzled and said, "You've got an appetite all of a sudden. What's come over you?"

By the time they were ready to go to church, the day was bright and clear. The freezing fog had vanished in the night, and the big winter sun made the icicles shine like glass and the snowy fields sparkle like Christmas glitter. All the way along the lane that led to the village, Irina looked happily about her at the blue shadows on the snow, the few crinkly brown leaves and stalks poking out of the frozen ditch, and the darting black shapes of birds looking for berries, and she thought to herself, I love Christmas!

Inside the church it was dark after the dazzling snow, but the crib in the corner was lit by glimmering candles. After the mass Irina went and knelt there, looking at the still figures kneeling in the hay. The Baby in the manger held out his stiff arms toward her, and Irina wished she were alone so that she could explain all about Bella, but more and more people were lining up behind her. She smiled at the donkey on his pile of straw and then dropped her coins into the box and lit a candle, liking the warm smell of the wax.

And after the cold tramp home there was the warm smell of Christmas dinner.

"I'm hungry!" Irina said, and again her parents looked surprised, but they didn't say anything.

After dinner her mother and father admired their little presents and then settled in their armchairs, their faces rosy with sleep after the long morning. Before their eyes were quite closed, Irina said, "Can I go out to the barn?"

"Mmmm . . ." was all her mother said, and her father gave a little startled grunt as if wondering who had spoken. So Irina wrapped herself up and went out.

She ran first to the barn to stroke Bella, and then she began fetching and carrying things across the yard. She fetched two heavy buckets of warm water, a cake of soap, an old sponge from under the sink in the dairy, and two old towels that hung behind the door of the cowshed. Then she crept back into the house and went upstairs to get her own comb. She needed a brush, too, but she didn't dare take her own hairbrush in case it got spoiled and her mother found out. As long as she didn't break the comb, she could wash it afterward, and no one would know.

Then she was ready to start work.

First she washed Bella's mane and tail, being as careful as she could not to let the soapy water get into the horse's eyes. She washed and rinsed and washed and rinsed, but the hair still felt coarse and greasy, and she had to fetch two more buckets of clean warm water and do it all again.

"I think it's clean now," she said, "but I'll need more water for your coat and your feet." And off she went again with the buckets. But when she started to wash Bella's coat, she got a surprise. She had thought that Bella would be made of painted wood like a rocking horse, but she wasn't.

"Your coat's real," she said, "just like your mane and tail. . . ."

She soaped it all over very carefully and rinsed away the dirty suds with the sponge. It was a real coat, all right, and though it was still wet, it looked as if it would be quite a pale color. Irina washed the horse's feet and then used the last bucket of clean water to sponge her face and ears very gently. Then she rubbed Bella all over with the towels and started work with her comb.

She combed the tail first and then the mane, holding the long hair and starting from the ends the way she did with her own hair, because that way it didn't hurt. It took a long time.

"There," she said at last. "All finished."

Then she remembered something.

She remembered her grandfather. At least, she didn't remember him exactly, because he had died when she was only a baby, but she remembered her father talking about him and how he had kept a pony and trap all his life.

Irina went to the far end of the barn where her father kept what he called "things that might come in useful" and her mother called "junk that ought to be thrown out." She began to look at everything carefully. She didn't know exactly what she was looking for, but if her grandfather had kept a pony, then there might just be something useful for Bella.

She was right. It took her a long time, and she bumped and scratched herself climbing over bits of old farm implements, and almost choked on the clouds of dust that flew up as

she pulled at pieces of torn sacking. But right at the back in the corner, weighed down by what looked like part of a plow, she discov- ered a wooden trunk with a broken metal lock.

The box was hemmed in by so many other things that she had no hope of getting it out, but she did manage to drag away the heavy piece of plow from the top and open it. It was impossible in the dark corner to see ex- actly what the box contained, but Irina felt inside and pulled the things out. One by one she climbed out with them to where she could see.

"Bella! Look!" she cried, examining her treasure. "There's everything for you, even a blanket!" And there was.

The blanket was old and far too big for Bella, but still it would keep her warm. And there were combs and brushes and bits of harnesses and reins whose leather had rotted away. Irina didn't know the use of half the things, but she put everything in a tidy pile in the corner behind Bella, except for the blanket.

The blanket she put carefully over Bella, who was still very wet. It was so big that she folded it double, and even then it covered the horse completely from head to tail.

"It doesn't look very nice," Irina explained, "but we have to keep you warm."

She stroked Bella's nose, which was all that was visible under the heavy blanket, and said, "Now you can have a long, long sleep until tomorrow."

When she came out of the barn, the winter sun was setting, huge and red, and all the snow was lit with a pink light.

Irina thought, It's almost the end of Christmas Day. But she didn't feel sad—she felt excited, as if instead of the end of something it was the beginning of something. And it was.

Five

"IRINA!" called her mother from the dairy. "Are you supposed to be helping or not? Irina!"

The sun glittered on the snow in the yard, but no answer came, and no Irina came either.

"Irina!" called her father like an echo. "Irina! Your mother's calling you!"

But still Irina didn't come.

The broken door of the big barn stood open, and the morning sun beamed in low, its light glittering with reflections from the snow. Inside the door, Irina stood holding the old blanket, her face as bright as the sunshine as she gazed in astonishment at the result of her work. She had hoped, when she took off the blanket that morning, that Bella would look clean and pretty, but she hadn't hoped for this.

Bella was beautiful. She stood there in the broad beam of sunlight, and her coat was smooth and fine, the color of the palest sand. Her mane and tail were as blond as Irina's long hair, glowing with gold and silver lights picked out by the morning sun. She no longer looked sad; she looked so sleek and elegant that Irina felt all her shyness come back, and she felt afraid to touch such a beautiful creature.

Very timidly, still clutching the blanket, she went closer, and she saw then that something was wrong. Bella was not perfect. Across her back there were marks, reddish marks like stripes. Irina forgot her shyness. She dropped the blanket and went closer still. Those marks were the marks of a whip!

"Oh, no . . . ," whispered Irina. She remembered the frightening story of Black Jack, who whipped and starved his horses. Had he been so cruel and stupid that he even whipped a horse that wasn't real and could do no work for him?

"Poor Bella." She knelt beside the horse

and put her arms around its neck, feeling the thick, silky mane against her cheek. "It must have hurt when I scrubbed and scrubbed at you, but I didn't know. I couldn't see under all that dirt. And now I don't know what to do. I could fetch some ointment for you, the sort we use if the cows hurt themselves out in the pasture—but I don't know if real ointment will work on a pretend horse. . . ."

"Irina! I won't tell you again!"

Irina scrambled to her feet.

"I have to go and help my mother—and I will bring some real ointment and try it."

She ran to the dairy and started working hard without a word, thinking all the time of Black Jack and his whip as though she were afraid he might come back to life.

"I don't know what's the matter with you," her mother said, after she'd told Irina to do something three times without getting an answer. "You look as though you're in a dream. There's no time for dreaming when there's work to be done."

Irina hardly heard her. All day she watched for the chance to get the ointment from the cowshed without anyone seeing. At last, when it was almost suppertime, she managed it. She ran to the barn with the big jar hidden under her coat.

The ointment was thick and had a strong smell. Very carefully Irina smoothed it over each of the angry red welts on Bella's back. Then she put her own clean handkerchief over the worst part. It wasn't really big enough, but it would help protect the sore parts from the rough, heavy blanket. She tidied the straw around Bella's feet and gave her a little kiss on the nose that was as soft and smooth as velvet. Then she said good-night.

For three days Irina put ointment on Bella's sore back, and each time she had to sneak the jar out of the cowshed without anyone seeing her and sneak it back in afterward. On the fourth day the marks were gone. On the fifth day she brought scissors and trimmed Bella's mane so that it didn't fall in her eyes so much. Every morning and every evening she brushed Bella's sandy-yellow coat and combed her silvery mane and tail, and on the sixth day, when Bella was quite perfect, Irina had an idea.

"I'll bring you some of the cows' hay," she said. "They won't mind." Her father would mind if he found out—Irina knew that. He'd let her have a bit of straw, but hay was much more expensive. Still, she would only take a little bit, and since Bella could only pretend to eat it, Irina wouldn't ever have to take any more.

So that night, when Irina said good-night to her, Bella had clean straw around her feet, a thick blanket to keep her warm, and a small heap of sweet-smelling hay in front of her.

Irina went to bed at nine o'clock. At first she couldn't get to sleep, although she had worked hard and was tired. A terrible blizzard had begun during supper. The wind howled and whined in the chimneys and flung the branches of the apple tree against her bedroom window, where snowflakes whirled and flew so thickly that they made her dizzy as she lay watching them.

Irina liked the snow when it fell softly, but the screaming wind frightened her and made her think again of Black Jack, the evil farmer. Even though she was warm and snug under her thick quilt, she shivered at the noise of the blizzard and hoped that Bella would be warm enough under her blanket. And at last, as she thought of Bella, her eyes closed and she fell asleep.

She slept heavily for a long time, and what it was that woke her she didn't know. One minute she was fast asleep, and the next minute she was sitting bolt upright in her bed, wide awake and staring at the window. It seemed to her that a sudden noise, like a door

banging, had woken her, but now everything was silent. The blizzard had stopped, as blizzards do, as suddenly as it had begun, and now the full moon was shining in at her window, bright and silvery in a starry sky.

Irina gazed at the moon, her body tense and her heart beating loud and fast. Something must have woken her, but now it was all quiet, too quiet. The black boughs of the apple tree were still, and yet something out there was moving—she was sure of it. A soft swishing noise—there *was* something! Then a muffled pattering noise!

Irina jumped out of bed and ran to the window. She pressed her forehead to the cold glass and looked down, her heart beating so loudly that it hurt. Down in the yard the big door of the barn stood open, and a beautiful horse, its mane flowing like quicksilver in the moonlight, was trotting swiftly around in wide circles in the snow.

Six

"BELLA!" CALLED IRINA SOFTLY. The beautiful horse stopped and tossed up her head. Then she spun around on her hind legs and trotted toward the sound of Irina's voice. Right beneath the window she stopped again and looked up, her whole body quivering. She stretched her head forward toward the ground and started to paw at it with her front hoof, striking the icy stones and shaking her silvery mane.

"I'm coming!" cried Irina, and she ran out of her room and down the stairs, swift and silent in her bare feet.

"Bella!" As soon as she saw Irina, the horse began trotting in circles again, her head turning this way and that as though she were looking for something. Suddenly she stopped beside the stump of a tree where Irina's father always chopped wood. She settled there, standing square on her four hooves, and turned her head toward Irina, waiting.

Irina understood at once. Without stopping to think of her bare feet and thin nightdress, without wondering whether she shouldn't feel afraid, she ran to the tree stump and climbed onto it, and in a moment she was on Bella's back and holding the streaming silver mane.

With a soft whinny of pleasure, Bella turned and cantered toward the farmyard gate. She checked and gathered herself and then leapt. Irina hardly felt the jump. It felt more like flying. Her cold bare feet clung to Bella's smooth warm sides, and her fingers entwined themselves in the thick mane, and they were off like the wind across the wide snowy fields.

The snow was so deep after the blizzard that Bella's hoofbeats were almost silent, and the moon was so big and bright that they could see for miles and miles. On and on they went, flying over hedges, fences, and ditches, speeding through copses where Irina had to rest her cheek on Bella's mane to avoid the snow-laden branches, then out again across the white fields in the moonlight. Irina didn't think to wonder where Bella was taking her. She didn't think of being frightened. She didn't think of being cold. She didn't think of anything. She felt the warmth of Bella's galloping body, the strong thick mane in her fingers, the ever-increasing speed that lifted her long hair and made it stream out behind like the horse's tail. More than anything else, she felt happy.

At last Bella began to turn in a wide circle. She jumped a low fence and galloped for home, and all too soon they were over the gate and back in the farmyard. Bella halted, and then walked quietly to the tree stump to let Irina slide down from her back. The horse was panting, and her breath was steamy in the night air.

Irina got down from the tree stump and went to stroke Bella's neck. Bella lowered her head and turned to nuzzle Irina's hair with her warm velvety nose. Then she trotted off into the barn and stood quietly in her corner on the straw. Irina hurried after her.

"I have to put your blanket on you. You're so hot from galloping, and now you'll be cold." She picked up the heavy blanket, but

no matter how she tried, she couldn't lift it onto Bella's back. She could only reach up to her shoulder. Bella turned to look at her, with big, gentle eyes, waiting patiently. Irina didn't know what to do. She tried again, but the blanket was so heavy and Bella was so tall that it was impossible.

"I can't reach you," she told Bella. "You were only small before, and now I can't reach."

Bella must have understood then. She began turning around and around in her corner, pawing and scraping at the straw beneath her feet. When it was smooth and flat, she knelt down very carefully and then lowered her hindquarters. Irina covered her with the blanket, and Bella at once sat up, straightened her front legs, and sprang upright, shaking herself.

Irina ran to fetch a bucket of water and some hay—"In case you get hungry and thirsty," she said, placing these in front of Bella. "Good-night." She reached up to stroke Bella's cheek, but the horse didn't lower her head and nuzzle her as Irina would have liked. She stood very still and straight, looking very serious, and slowly raised her left front hoof.

"What is it, Bella? I don't understand. Have you hurt it?" Bella went on standing with her foot raised for a long time. Then, seeing that Irina did nothing, she put it down and lifted the right one, still looking straight ahead and waiting. She lifted each of her four feet in turn. Perhaps, in the end, she understood that Irina didn't know what to do, so she bent to nuzzle her as if to say good-night.

Irina ran into the house and climbed the stairs. As she crept past her parents' bedroom, she heard her father snoring. She ran to her own room and jumped into bed, snuggling down under the quilt. She was so happy that she fell asleep at once to dream of riding over the snowy fields with Bella.

"Irina? Irina!"

Irina opened her eyes and sat up. It was morning, and her mother was calling her.

"Irina! I've been calling you for the last half hour!"

But Irina didn't move at once. She was trying to remember something. Something had happened. She felt different today. Then she remembered her dream of riding over the snow. Could a dream make her feel so happy and so different? She got up and dressed quickly. The dream was still whirling around in her head, making her feel confused. She ran downstairs and through the kitchen toward the back door.

"Irina!" her mother said. "Where do you think you're going? You're already too late to help me with the hens, and now breakfast's ready."

"I just want to go out for one minute, please—"

"Sit down," her mother said. "Your father's already in from milking."

Her father walked into the kitchen, and Irina sat down at the table. They didn't usually talk much at breakfast. A lot of work had already been done, and a lot more was waiting to be done, and so they ate in a hurry. But this morning Irina's father had something to tell them.

"That was a fair blizzard we had last night," he began. "There are drifts as high as a man in some parts." He chewed in silence for a moment, then gulped at his drink, frowning. "It's a funny thing, but all over the yard there are prints in the fresh snow."

Irina's mother put down the plate she was about to carry away.

"Don't tell me a fox—"

"No. You don't need to start fretting about your hens. There's nothing missing, and besides, they weren't a fox's prints."

"What, then?"

Irina stared silently at her plate as they talked, her heart beating faster and faster, her face growing redder and redder.

"A horse, I reckon."

It wasn't a dream. It *wasn't*.

"Are you sure?" her mother said. "I don't see how a horse could have got in with the five-barred gate shut."

"Jumped it," her father said, getting up to go out with a full, steaming mug still in his hand. "There's a wild herd passes this way twice a year, but it's early days for them yet. The streams are all still frozen. There were some other prints as well, but I couldn't make them out."

"It was Bella!" said Irina, suddenly breaking her silence.

"And who's Bella?" asked her father, standing his mug on the end of the dresser near the door and sitting down to pull on his boots.

"My horse. She ... last night I ..." Her

51

voice trailed off, and she looked down at her plate again, wishing she hadn't said anything.

"Irina, clear the table," her mother said.

"But it *was* Bella," Irina insisted quietly.

"You listen to me, young lady," said her mother sharply. "Making up stories at your age means telling lies. You're not a two-year-old. Clear that table. And I've had enough of you messing in that barn half the day when there's work to be done. If there's any more of it, I'll pitch that worm-eaten old thing out."

"Now, now," interrupted her father mildly, "leave her be. It's something for her to play with. She'll forget about it when school starts." And he went out.

Irina helped clear the table and wash the dishes in silence. And all the time she was thinking to herself, It's not a lie. If they go in the barn, they'll see! They'll *see*. . . .

But first she had to see for herself. She had to escape from her mother's watchful eyes. It was a long time before she managed it, but at last she got out into the yard and ran to open the door of the old barn.

"Bella . . . ?"

She was there in her corner, small and still,

almost buried in the blanket that was far too big for her. Irina's heart was filled with confusion and disappointment. She knelt beside the little horse and turned back the big blanket to stroke her mane. Then she saw that the hay was gone and the water bucket was empty.

Seven

BELLA WAS REAL. Whatever happened to her in the daytime, at night she was real. Dreams don't eat hay and drink water. Dreams don't leave hoofprints in the snow.

Every night Irina went to bed as early as she could and slept happily until Bella came to wake her, knowing that when the moon was high, she would hear the noise of hooves striking on the icy stones in the yard. Then she would run to the window and see Bella waiting for her out in the white moonlit world of night.

They rode far and fast, as free as birds, and during their journeys Irina never spoke a word. She clung to Bella with her toes and fingers, her eyes bright and her hair streaming behind her as they flew across the snowy fields like the wind.

She never tried again to tell her parents the truth. She knew it would only make them angry. And yet she had to tell somebody—not just for the sake of telling, because Irina was an only child and used to keeping her secrets to herself, but because she was worried about something. Each night after their ride, when Bella trotted back into the barn, she continued to lift up each of her feet in turn, waiting. Irina had to ask someone what it meant.

Then she remembered the blind man. He knew all about Bella, and he had said Irina could come back and see him whenever she wanted. Her chance came when school started. One day a week, Irina's mother came to school to meet her and they did some shopping. Irina waited until they were in a long line in the grocer's, which was only a step away from the blind man's junk shop.

"Can I go out and look in the shop windows?" Irina asked.

"If you like—but stay on this side of the square where I can find you."

"I will!" Irina went as fast as she could and then paused at the gloomy entrance to the junk shop. Would the blind man recognize her footsteps and call out the way he did with that boy on Christmas Eve? No sound came from inside.

"Can I come in?" asked Irina timidly, taking a step forward.

"Of course you can," came the voice of the blind man.

Irina knocked the snow from her boots and went toward the big carved armchair. The blind man was sitting there just as before, as if he had never moved since Irina last saw him.

"And how is little Irina?" he asked.

"Did you recognize my steps?"

"No," said the blind man, "you haven't been to see me often enough for that, but I never forget a voice. And are you happy now with Bella?"

"Yes, I am," Irina said, and then she hesitated, wondering if he would believe her if she told the truth.

After a moment's silence the blind man said, "You might as well tell me, now that you've come." Just as though, blind as he was, he could see into her thoughts. So Irina told him the truth about her night rides.

"So Bella *must* be a real horse," she said at the end. "And she's mine, all mine, and that's why I'm happy, only what am I to do about her feet? There's nobody else I can ask except you."

"Give me your hand," the blind man said, lifting his own pale, mouselike hands toward her. Irina gave him her hand.

"What you say is not true," he said gravely.

"But she is real, she *is!*" protested Irina, tears of disappointment filling her eyes. "I thought you would understand. I thought you knew about Bella."

"Bella is God's creature," the blind man said sternly.

"You don't believe me!"

"Many people believe what you believe," the blind man said, "and all of them are unhappy just as you will be unhappy if you go on believing what is false." He lifted his hand to her cheek. "You're crying, but you'll shed bitter tears before long if you don't listen to what I tell you. Never say what is false. Never say that any creature on this earth is yours. Now, go behind my chair to where there's a big chest and take the package that's lying there. It's for you. You see, I was expecting you."

Irina went to the big chest and took the package that was lying on its dusty surface.

"Thank you," she said, but she was still crying tears of disappointment because he didn't believe her. She tried to dry her eyes on the back of her glove and made one last try.

"Couldn't a spell have been put on Bella to stop her being real, to save her from Black Jack so that he couldn't hurt her anymore? Couldn't that be what happened?"

"There's a book in that package," the blind man said, without answering her. "Read it carefully. And if you want to go on being happy, remember my words. Never deceive yourself into believing something that isn't true."

Irina ran out of the junk shop and said to herself that she would never, *never* go there again. Grown-ups were all alike, and it was useless to tell them anything. It was better to talk just to Bella. Even if Bella couldn't answer, she always understood. And as soon as they got home, Irina did talk to Bella for as long as she could before supper.

"I don't care any more if nobody believes me," she told Bella, stroking her mane. "From now on, I'm only going to tell my secrets to you."

She quite forgot about the package until she was going up to bed. She saw it lying on the chair where she had dropped it when she came in, and though she hated the blind man now, she couldn't help being curious about what was in it.

Upstairs, she settled down in bed and untied the string on the package. It was a book, as the blind man had said, and not a nice-looking book either. It was old, and its hard red cover had faded to a grayish pink. Its spine was broken, and some of the pages had come loose. One of these slipped out and fell from the bed to the floor, but not before Irina had noticed that there was a picture on it. A picture of a horse.

She reached down to pick it up. The horse in the picture was standing with one foot raised, and a man was bending over the foot with what looked like a paintbrush in his hand. Quickly Irina opened the book to its title page and read *Feeding, Grooming, and Training Your Horse.*

Then the blind man had believed her, in spite of everything he'd said. He must have

believed her if he gave her a book that would help her look after Bella!

Irina wasted no time wondering why he should have behaved so strangely. She started to read the book as fast as she could. It had been written for adults, not for anyone as young as Irina, and there were many words in it that she couldn't understand. Even so, there were plenty of pictures to help her, and she recognized a lot of the things she had found in her grandfather's trunk.

Later that night, when they had ridden as far as they felt like riding over the snow and were back in the barn, Irina knew what she had to do when Bella stood patiently holding up her foot. At least she thought she did. She was ready with all the right implements from the pile of her grandfather's things in the corner, and she knew she had to scrape the stones and dirt from under Bella's hoof and wipe it clean and then paint hoof grease on it with a brush.

But learning practical things from a book by yourself is not the best way of learning, and it was lucky for Irina that she had a teacher on hand—Bella. Bella might not know how to speak, but she knew just what had to be done and how it should be done. She gave Irina her left front foot and turned to watch her as she worked, nuzzling her back every so often to encourage her. Irina's first attempt was slow, but at last she straightened up and said, "There, that's one finished." She went around to Bella's right and waited for the right foot to be offered to her, but nothing happened.

"You have to give me your right foot now, Bella."

Bella stood still. What could be wrong? Every night Bella had offered her feet one by one, first at the front, then at the back.

"Bella?" Irina looked up at her, stroking her neck. "What is it?" But Bella only stood there, tall and pale and elegant, gazing straight ahead, blinking her big soft eyes. At last Irina remembered that the pictures in the book showed the man always working from the horse's left side. She went back to where she had stood before, and Bella at once lifted her right foot and held it toward Irina, behind the left. Irina got to work again, and Bella turned and nuzzled her back to tell her she was doing it right.

When all four hooves were clean and shiny, Bella knelt to have her blanket put on, and Irina brought her hay and water and said good-night.

Just before she fell asleep in her warm bed, Irina thought, Perhaps one day, when she feels well and safe again, Bella will be a real horse all the time.

And she was right.

Eight

THERE WAS A TIME, before she had Bella, when Irina always walked sadly home after school, knowing that all the other children would be running in and out of one another's houses in the village or perhaps skating on the big pond nearby. Irina had never been allowed to stay and play. The winters were so long, and darkness came down so quickly, that her mother had always made her come straight home. And so she had always gone sadly on her way, looking back sometimes when she heard the others calling to one another and laughing.

But now it was different. Irina was always first out of the school gate, her long braid bobbing and swinging as she ran toward the long lane that led toward home and Bella. She would arrive red-cheeked and out of breath, and hurry straight into the big barn, calling, "Bella! I'm home!"

Then she would brush Bella's coat and comb her mane and chatter to her about everything that had happened at school that day, sure that the little horse was listening to every word. Then, at night, when Bella was her real tall beautiful self, they would ride.

One night, when the ice was creaking on the roofs and the streams bubbling under the snow, Bella galloped much farther away than usual. Instead of making a big circle and then heading for home, she went on and on, faster and faster over the flat snowy fields toward the horizon. Then, very suddenly, she stopped dead, her head lifted and her whole body tense and quivering.

"What is it?" Irina asked. "Bella, what is it?"

Bella remained rigid, her ears pricked. Had she heard something? Smelled something? Irina clung to Bella's quivering body and looked about her at the miles of snowy fields, the velvety sky dotted thickly with stars, the silver moon. She could see no danger. Then she wondered if they were near Black Jack's old farm. She had no idea where it was, but then, they had come so far that she didn't recognize anything.

"Bella," she whispered, shivering and clutching tighter at the long mane, "let's go home. I'm frightened."

But Bella didn't hear or turn to nuzzle Irina's toes. She didn't move, and Irina could feel the horse's great heart beating so fast and loudly that it seemed as if it must burst. Still Bella stared, her eyes fixed on the horizon. She whinnied, almost under her breath, then relaxed. Whatever she had heard or smelled was gone. She turned her head to nuzzle Irina's cold toes with her warm nose and then took off at a gallop for home.

The next night the same thing happened, but it was even more frightening. When she saw that Bella was galloping on toward the horizon instead of turning for home, Irina called to her over the noise of the wind their galloping made, "Don't go so far away, Bella! Please don't!"

But Bella galloped on until she came to the same spot where she had stopped the night before. Again she stood rigid and trembling, with her big eyes fixed on the horizon and her big heart beating faster and faster. Her breath came in sharp snorts.

"Bella! You're frightening me! Bella!"

But Bella seemed to have forgotten that anyone was riding her at all. She spun around suddenly, then back again. She ran to the left, swung herself around on her hindquarters and ran to the right, then swung around again, and always with her eyes fixed on the horizon. Irina clung on as well as she could, but she slid sideways at each violent turn, and only Bella's long mane saved her from falling. She surely would have fallen sooner or later, but, just as she had the night before, Bella suddenly relaxed, breathed normally, and turned to gallop for home.

The third night, Irina was almost afraid to go out. But when she looked down from her window and saw Bella waiting patiently by the tree stump, quiet and composed as if nothing had happened, she summoned the courage to go down and mount her.

When they reached the field where they always used to turn for home, Irina said, "Let's go back now, Bella! Please let's go back." But Bella only galloped faster until she reached that same spot and stopped. She

trembled so much that Irina started to trem-
ble, too, and again the horse ran back and
forth, back and forth, watching the horizon,
her ears pricked, snorting sharply.

"What can you hear, Bella, *what*?"

Then Irina heard, too. At first it was a
distant, muted rumbling, like a thunderstorm
far away. It came closer and closer, and Bella's heart beat faster and louder. Then Irina
understood. Hoofbeats. Hundreds and hundreds of hoofbeats, and on the horizon she
saw the wild horses streaming along at full
gallop, their manes as white as the snow.

Bella threw up her head and neighed, a
long, high, desperate call that was almost a
scream. From far away came an answering
call. Bella reared, pawing the air, then
plunged. Irina felt herself thrown into space
with the snow and the sky spinning upside
down, and then the white ground hit her
hard and everything turned black and silent.

When Irina opened her eyes again, she felt
sick and dizzy, and her mouth and ears were
full of snow. She got to her feet very slowly,
staring at the empty horizon, her ears buzzing
in the silence. Then she turned and started
walking home. Her feet were bare in the

snow, but she didn't notice the cold. She knew that one of her hands was hurt badly, but she didn't feel the pain; she just knew in her head that it was there. She was very far from home, but she felt no fear of getting lost. She knew that she must go on putting one foot in front of the other, but she felt nothing at all. And she never once turned to look back after the wild horses who had taken Bella away.

Nine

IRINA LAY VERY STILL IN HER BED. Her face was white except for a reddish purple bruise on her forehead. Her right arm rested outside the quilt with a stiff bandage around the wrist. She wasn't asleep; her eyes were wide open. Outside the door of her bedroom, her parents were talking to the doctor in low voices.

"It's just the shock. . . . You'll see that in a few days. . . . No serious injury . . ."

"Sleepwalking . . . She must have . . . We found her early in the morning on a pile of straw in the barn. . . ."

"Just keep her quiet, and don't worry. . . ."

Irina could hear them, but she didn't listen. Inside her head, everything was empty and silent. The sun was shining outside the window, and the snow was melting and dripping from the black boughs of the apple tree. Irina closed her eyes and slept.

After a while, Irina was sent back to school. She was very quiet and well behaved as usual, but she didn't learn anything. At home, she answered when she was spoken to, but if no one spoke to her she was silent. Her parents looked at her and then at each other. They called the doctor.

The doctor looked at Irina's eyes and throat and squeezed her neck behind her ears. He said perhaps she was growing too much and gave her some bitter medicine. But Irina wasn't growing. She didn't grow one inch taller, and her hair didn't grow one inch longer. The doctor said perhaps she was studying too much. But Irina wasn't studying at all. Every evening she took her books and sat by the window. The black boughs of the apple tree grew buds that opened into tiny leaves of the palest green. Irina watched the leaves unfold, and inside her head everything was empty and silent.

The sun grew warmer, and the cows were turned out into the pasture. In the evenings, Irina was sent to drive them home to be milked. Afterward she sat by the open window with her book and watched the thick white apple blossoms ruffled by the warm breeze that filled her room with their perfume, and inside her head everything was empty and silent.

The tree grew small green apples. By the time they were big and red, the air had turned bright and cold. Irina helped her father pick the apples. They had always picked the apples together, even when Irina was so small that she could only stand at the foot of the tree with the basket.

When he remembered how she used to enjoy it and saw how pale and thin she looked now, her father felt sorry for her and said, "How would you like it if I bought you a little dog? It would be company for you, something to play with."

"No, thank you," Irina said. "I don't want a dog."

"But it might cheer you up," her father said. "It would be your very own dog, and you could look after it yourself."

"No!" cried Irina. "I don't want one."

"But why?"

"Because it would run away! I'd look after it and love it, and then it would run away!" And she scrambled down from the apple tree and went to shut herself in her bedroom.

Soon the apple tree was bare, and its branches tapped and rattled at Irina's window, shaken by the first winter wind. Irina sat watching as she had watched through all the other seasons. Inside her head, everything was empty and silent, and never once in all that time, even in her deepest, most secret thoughts, had she said or thought the name Bella. Never once had she shed a single tear.

One night Irina and her parents were having supper in the kitchen. Over the noise of the roaring wood stove a faint moan could be heard in the chimneys.

"That's a north wind," Irina's father said. "Next thing you know, it'll start snowing. Once the wild horses have gone through, you can count on snow starting, like clockwork."

"Wild horses?" Irina's fork clattered onto her plate. Her face had turned red.

"They come by this way in the spring, as soon as the snow begins to melt," her father said, "but you've never seen them. They pass too far away from here—but don't you remember that one of them once got into the yard, and I found hoofprints in the snow? They'll be on their way back to their winter pastures any day now, mark my words, and the minute they've gone it'll start snowing."

Every night, after her father's words, Irina watched by her window. She no longer pretended to read. There was no book in her lap. She sat there rigid and still, her eyes fixed on the horizon, the emptiness in her head beating to one repeating rhythm: "Don't let it snow yet. Don't let it snow yet." Sometimes, exhausted by the waiting, she fell asleep with her forehead against the cold windowpane.

Each night she waited, and each day the sky grew duller and grayer and heavier. Then, one evening, as she sat there in the twilight, she saw something twirl slowly down between the branches of the apple tree. It was a snowflake. Another fell, and another, and as the evening darkened into night, the silent snow fell faster and thicker until there was nothing but whirling snowflakes to be seen.

Then the empty silence in Irina's head was flooded with memories of snowy rides and moonlit fields, of a flowing mane and a warm velvety nose that nuzzled her feet, of the thunder of hooves and her fall through the air to the hard cold ground.

"Bella!" It was the first time since that night that she had said Bella's name. Now she wrenched open the window, calling and calling as though her heart would break, "Bella! Bella! Bella!"

The north wind whirled the snowflakes into the room, touching her face with icy kisses, and Irina began to cry in loud, broken sobs as she understood at last what the blind man had told her.

"Never say that any creature on this earth is yours, or you'll shed bitter tears."

Ten

IT WAS A HARD WINTER THAT YEAR. Hard for the fox who prowled around the locked chicken sheds at night, his ribs showing through his tattered fur. Hard for the small birds who fell frozen from their branches into the snow. Hard, too, for Irina. She had cried until she had no more tears left to shed, and then decided that if she couldn't be happy, she could try to be good. She tried to talk more to her mother and keep her company during her long hours of work, and when her father made little jokes to cheer her up she smiled. At school she worked twice as hard as the others to make up for being so behind. But as she walked home alone each afternoon, leaving the shouting and laughter of the village children behind, her heart was as heavy as the gray, snow-burdened sky, and it seemed to her that the winter would never end.

But winter always does end, and one night, as Irina slept, the ice on the roof creaked and slid, slid and creaked, until, toward dawn, a great slice of it thundered down into the yard.

Irina opened her eyes. The room was lit with a cold pink light. The sun was only just over the horizon, and the melting snow was reflecting its light. She heard a thin trickle of water in the eaves, and another patch of ice dislodged itself and began to slide. Then she heard hooves striking on the icy stones in the yard.

Irina got up and went cautiously to the window, almost afraid to look down. Bella was there. She was standing very still now, watching and listening, her coat and mane reflecting the same cool pink light as the snow. Irina went downstairs. She put her thick coat over her nightdress and pushed her feet into her warm boots. She was trying to keep calm, but her heart was thumping loudly.

"Bella . . ."

Bella allowed Irina to stroke her neck, but then she broke away and trotted swiftly to the old barn. The broken door was ajar. Irina started to follow her.

"Bella? Have you come home?"

But before Irina could follow her inside the barn, Bella burst out again, trotted straight toward her, nuzzled her chest, then spun around, jumped the five-barred gate, and galloped at a desperate speed toward the horizon.

"Bella! No! Bella!" Irina ran as far as the gate and then stood watching until the galloping form was no longer visible. Bella was gone.

"What's going on? What's all this noise?" Irina's father came out of the kitchen door, half-dressed, his hair hanging over his eyes. "Irina!"

Irina turned, but her father was no longer looking at her; he was looking down at the hoofprints in the melting snow, and now he followed them into the barn.

"Well, I never . . . Irina! Irina! Come and look!"

Irina looked back once more at the sun rising over the flat, empty fields. Then she went to her father.

He was standing just inside the barn door near the corner where Bella used to live. Irina had never been in there since, and she didn't want to go in there now, but her father insisted. He took her by the shoulders. "Look, Irina!"

The straw she had put down for Bella last year was still there. And standing on the straw was a foal, a tiny perfect replica of Bella.

"It's a female, and a little beauty," said her father quietly. The foal was too weak and exhausted to look up at them. It took all the little energy it had just to stay on its wobbling legs, and one of them, its right hind leg, was lifted slightly off the floor.

"Why, it's lame," her father said, bending to look closer. "Got tangled up in some wire. . . ." He untwisted the wire carefully. "It'll leave a scar, but it should mend. That's why its mother abandoned it, but why she brought it here is a mystery."

Irina stood where she was, her face hard and angry.

"Why did she leave it? She should have looked after it if it was lame. Why?"

"They have to keep up," her father said. "If they can't keep up, the mothers are forced to leave them by the rest of the herd. She must have had a desperate run to get it here and then catch up with them . . . if she did catch up with them." He patted the little blond mane. "Well, I don't think you've much of a chance, little one, unless Irina wants to try giving you some milk from a bottle. . . ."

"No! I won't love it! I won't look after it! I won't!"

"Well, please yourself," her father said. "I thought you might like to have a horse that would be your very own."

Irina ran out of the barn and shut herself in her bedroom. When she came down to breakfast, her face was still pale and angry. Her father was talking about the foal, and her mother said, "There's the baby's bottle we use when there's a weak calf born, I suppose. . . ."

But Irina didn't say anything.

Her father finished his breakfast and put his boots back on. "It'll be dead by the end of the day," he said, and went out.

It wasn't a school day. Irina helped her mother in the house and then in the dairy. They were skimming cream and filling little tubs with it. Irina's mother glanced at the shelf where they kept the baby's bottle for the calves and said, "There's no understanding you, Irina. Last year you spent every hour God sends messing in that barn with a toy horse, and now there's that poor creature in there and you won't even look at it. . . ."

Irina went on working in silence, but her face got paler and paler, and her father's words kept repeating themselves in her head: "It'll be dead by the end of the day."

She saw Bella galloping desperately, her brave heart bursting with the effort to save her foal and her own life, felt Bella nuzzling her chest, trusting her to help. . . .

Suddenly the little tub fell from her hand and rolled across the dairy floor. She ran to get the baby's bottle and clutched at her mother's arm. "Some milk for it! Give me some milk for it!"

"We'll take it warm from the cow," her mother said. "That might help."

The foal had given up its struggle to stand on three legs. It was lying on the straw, its eyes almost closed. Irina knelt down beside it and held the teat of the bottle near its lips, but it was too weak to lift its head. She squeezed a few warm drops into its mouth.

"Don't die," she pleaded. "Please don't die! I'll look after you and love you. I'll take you out in the meadow, where there'll be grass and flowers and a stream to cool your feet. And when you're big and strong enough, you'll be free—you'll be your own self. I'll never say you're mine, but please don't die."

She slid her hand beneath the little head and lifted it gently to cradle it against herself. Feeling the warmth, the foal pushed its soft nose against her breast and opened its eyes. It looked dazed, as though wondering where it was, but when Irina pushed the teat near its mouth, it began to suck.

Eleven

LOVED AND CARED FOR BY IRINA, the foal grew, and the lame leg mended. Her pale sandy-colored coat and silvery mane were so exactly like her mother's that, almost without thinking about it, Irina called her Bella. When the last of the snow had melted and the sun warmed the new grass, she led Bella out into the meadow.

Bella looked about her at the fresh green world, and her velvet nose twitched at all the scents coming to her on the warm breeze. With a little whinny of happiness, she began to run up and down the meadow, jumping and kicking and sometimes tumbling over on her too-long legs. Then she ran to Irina to nuzzle her.

"Do you like it, Bella? Do you?"

But Bella whirled around and was away

again, galloping around the meadow until she had no breath to gallop any more, and she settled to crop the sweet grass near Irina's feet.

Irina was growing, too. Once she was old enough to please herself, she began to call at the blind man's shop after school sometimes. Now that they understood each other, he was the person she most liked to talk to about Bella and how she was growing tall and beautiful and strong. She called on him so often that he soon learned to recognize her footsteps. One day he lifted his small, mouselike hand to touch Irina's smiling face and said, "I think you are growing tall and beautiful, too, Irina, just like your Bella." But Irina saw the little smile on his blind face and said, "Bella is God's creature, not mine."

The years passed, and Bella grew big and strong enough to carry Irina. One afternoon in autumn, when they had ridden far from home and it was time to turn back, Bella suddenly stopped cropping the grass and lifted her head, her ears pricked.

"What is it, Bella?" Irina asked gently, stroking her neck. But she knew what it was, and she slid down from the saddle and stood beside the horse's quivering body, waiting. She heard the thunder of hooves, and then the herd came into view, streaming across the horizon in the autumn mist. Let her be with them and safe, she thought, and then she looked up at Bella's tense body. She didn't speak to her or try to turn her away; she only watched and waited.

Bella's head was thrown high and still, her ears picking up every sound, her nostrils every scent. She was excited, and her heartbeat was loud and fast, but her big eyes looked puzzled, as though she was trying to connect the thundering hooves and the scent of the herd with a distant memory, a memory of a world that was all white, a terrible pain, a terrifying flight across the emptiness, and a warm nuzzle urging her on. But it was all so long ago that the memory faded with the fading of the hoofbeats. Bella relaxed and lowered her head to go on cropping the grass.

"Let's go home," Irina said, stroking her long smooth neck gently. "It's going to snow."

It was that same day that Irina's mother and father settled an argument that had been going on between them for years. They put on their oldest clothes and rolled up their

sleeves and went into the old barn to decide once and for all what were the "things that might come in useful" and what was "junk that ought to be thrown out." They were still in there, arguing over part of a rusty old plow, when Irina and Bella came back from their ride.

Perhaps it was all that dusty junk that reminded him of the blind man's shop, or perhaps it was the sound of the horse's hooves coming into the yard, but Irina's father sud-

denly laughed and said, "Do you remember that Christmas when Irina insisted on having a moth-eaten old toy horse for a present?"

"She was a strange one at that age," her mother said.

"She was, but she turned out all right in the end. I was just wondering, though, whatever happened to that horse."

"I forget," her mother said. "She probably got bored with it in the end and threw it out."